DISNEY
✦PRINCESS
Jasmine

Published by Ladybird Books Ltd.,
80 Strand, London WC2R 0RL
A Penguin Company
Penguin Books Australia Ltd., Camberwell, Victoria, Australia
Penguin Books (NZ) Ltd., Private Bag 102902, NSMC, Auckland, New Zealand

2 4 6 8 10 9 7 5 3 1

Printed in China

Jasmine
The Search for Love

Ladybird

One day, Princess Jasmine was strolling in the palace gardens when she realised that Rajah, her pet tiger, wasn't with her. When she saw that the gate was open, Jasmine gasped. Rajah was gone!

"How will I ever find him?" she cried.

Then Jasmine remembered a magic carpet ride she had taken with one of her suitors. They had been able to see for miles!

"I must find the prince," she decided.

*D*isguising herself in a shawl, Jasmine quickly set out to look for the prince.

In the marketplace, she met Aladdin, a boy who had once helped her before. Jasmine explained her problem to him.

"I'll find the prince for you!" said Aladdin. "Wait on your balcony tonight."

Jasmine thanked him and headed home. She didn't realise that the prince she was looking for was really Aladdin!

*A*fter dinner that evening, Jasmine rushed straight to her balcony.

Sure enough, Prince Ali soon appeared out of the night sky on his magic carpet!

"I'm here to help!" he announced, bringing the carpet down close.

Delighted, Jasmine climbed aboard. Smiling at the prince, she noticed how kind and gentle his eyes were – and how much he looked like Aladdin!

Jasmine and Prince Ali sailed across the moonlit sky. Together, they looked down upon the city of Agrabah.

The scene was breathtaking. Jasmine was enchanted as she took in the city's twinkling lights and busy streets, with the majestic mountains beyond.

But Jasmine's beloved tiger, Rajah, was nowhere to be seen.

Soon the magic carpet left the city and swooped out over the forest. The trees shimmered in the silvery moonlight, making the forest look like a fairyland.

As they soared over a clearing, Jasmine suddenly gasped. She could see the orange and black stripes of a tiger glowing in the shadowy moonlight!

"Look!" cried Jasmine happily. "That must be Rajah!"

*P*rince Ali steered the carpet down towards the wandering tiger. As they got closer, Jasmine saw that it wasn't Rajah at all, but a female tiger.

The tiger rushed up to them, making soft growling noises and turning her head.

"Do you think she's trying to tell us something?" whispered Jasmine.

"Yes," Prince Ali whispered back. "Perhaps we'd better follow her."

*T*he tiger led them to a little stream. There, lying on the bank, was Rajah!

Jasmine rushed up to him joyfully and threw her arms around his neck.

"I've found you!" she cried. Rajah licked her face, but then held out his paw. There was a long, sharp thorn stuck in it.

"That's why you couldn't come home!" Jasmine gasped. Gently, she eased out the thorn, then calmed Rajah as best she could.

Rajah was ready to go home now. He looked sadly towards his new friend and nuzzled her neck in thanks.

"You can visit any time you like," Jasmine promised him. "Just let me know you're going – and look out for thorns!"

As Jasmine headed for home with Rajah and Aladdin, she found herself hoping that she would also be seeing more of her own new friend the prince, or was it Aladdin she was thinking of? She couldn't be sure!